Publisher's Note: This is a work of fiction. Names, characters, places, and incidents are a product of the author's imagination. Locales and public names are sometimes used for atmospheric purposes. Any resemblance to actual people, living or dead, or to businesses, companies, events, institutions, or locales is coincidental.

Edited by Aquila Editing

Cover Designer: Cormar Covers

HELLO FROM ABBY!

Thanks for picking up my book! If you want to check out more of my titles, please visit my author page at www.authorabbyknox.com

Happy reading!

V-CARD VACATION

FILTHY DIRTY SUMMER

ABBY KNOX

SUMMARY

Bree

I'm the last one of my friends who's still a virgin. At the age of 28, I've stopped looking for a Mister Right who makes my heart pound; I'll settle for a Mister Right Now to show up pound it out with me. No strings attached. So when my best friend books a girls trip to a remote island resort, it's the perfect opportunity to have one quick fling with a stranger. If I'm not good in bed? No problem! I never have to see him again. Too bad my hot diving instructor didn't get the "no strings attached" memo. Cody agrees to take care of my little problem, but he's creating a bigger situation by trying to get to know me. Why is he bothering to remember my likes and dislikes? He knows this is a sure thing. Well, too bad if he gets attached to me, because a long distance relationship is not part of my plan.

Cody

I love my job here on the islands. I've got my family, friends, and access to the most beautiful coral reefs in the world. There's only one piece missing to my puzzle. I want to settle down. I've been waiting my whole life for just the right one. What can I say? I'm a hopeless romantic who's looking for my lightning-bolt connection. I'd thought until today that I'd have to leave the islands to get my wish. When resort guest, Bree, dives into my life, I know I'm sunk. She's my lightning bolt, but all she wants is a quick jump start. Although I've agreed to help her with one tiny, minuscule problem and then never speak of it again, I just know that I'm not going to hold up most of that bargain. I'll help her, but I already know we're too good together for just a one night stand.

Welcome to a filthy dirty summer!

Drop it like it's hot with your 17 favorite instalove authors! Each stand-alone story delivers a scorching, fantasy-fueled romance!

No need to pack a swimsuit—your kindle is all you need for a wet and wild summer!

ONE

Bree

I TRAVEL thousands of miles to soak up the sunshine in the Pearl Crescent Islands only to be trapped in the middle of a lightning storm. Figures.

"Gonna steer into that crevasse; find us some cover."

Those authoritative words are spoken by Cody, my reef diving instructor, with serene confidence. His lazy smile has not faded with the appearance of the blue-gray thunderhead on the horizon. Nor have his unreadable blue eyes changed one iota as lightning slashes through the distant, darkening skies.

"By crevasse, you don't mean cave, right?" I pick at a snag on my beach towel, where it's folded in my lap. I should have stashed it somewhere to keep it dry, but I've been gripping it like a security blanket ever since the water became choppy. The towel was a personalized gift from my friends, who ordered it printed with a photo of my dog

Buster. I imagine he'd be trying to herd us to safety if he were here.

Cody and I cut short what was supposed to be a two-hour snorkeling adventure. I did see some fantastic things: turtles, and fish in every color of the rainbow. A stingray swam under me, brushing my tummy with its wide, sleek body. That made my whole life. Although I may have trained myself not to flinch at the possibility of being touched by a marine animal, that experience still electrified me.

And now, I'm going to be electrified—or electrocuted—if we don't get out of here. Just one problem. I'm terrified of caves. And there's nothing else nearby.

"Uh, yeah. I do mean a cave." Cody answers, yanking the cord on the motor of our little boat. "We can stay there until the storm calms down."

My hands sweat. I'm not yet close to the cave entrance of this tiny landmass rising out of the ocean, and I'm starting to feel discomfort.

Pursing my lips, I suck in a breath, then let it out slowly, like a leaky tire.

"Are you okay, Bree?"

Cody says this as if I'm a friend and not one of a dozen faceless guests at the Cerulean Resort and Spa that he has to shepherd from Little Loggerhead Island to the reef every week.

He's stopped working on the boat motor to watch me. I wonder what I must look like: a frizzy-haired chicken wringing her beach towel and darting her eyes around for any sign of shelter that does not resemble a deep, dark hole in the side of a cliff.

Wait. Why did he stop messing with the motor?

"I-I'm okay," I breathe, stuttering.

I paid a lot of money for this once-in-a-lifetime trip. I only had two goals other than relaxing on the beach and feeding coconut rum into my veins, preferably via an IV. With the slim pickings of single straight male resort guests, I struck out on achieving one goal. When I stepped on the little island-hopper plane in Pearl City, I thought I was luck, as the pilot, Austin, was ruggedly handsome. Alas, pilot Austin also had a little photograph of a hot blonde babe taped to his instrument panel.

Sigh.

Would the goddess of single female travelers please have mercy on me and push the cloud away for another couple of hours? Let me get my money's worth out of my reef adventure?

Sadly, that's not how weather works. I knew this going in. When I booked this trip, I also knew I had no control over who else might be populating the remote Pearl Crescent Islands simultaneously. That there might be zero candidates to help me punch my V-card was a known risk.

"You don't look okay," Cody says, crossing from the motor to the side of the boat to where I'm now standing, unsure what to do with myself in this emergency.

Getting control of my breathing, I lift the corner of my mouth in a smirk and try sarcasm. That always helps, doesn't it? "A wetsuit doesn't look great on everyone, but I thought I was making it work for you," I say.

Did I just flirt with Cody? With a man so far out of my league that I'm not allowed to play the same sport as him?

Cody huffs a dry laugh.

And I just made him uncomfortable. Because of course I did. Why would he take that as a compliment from me? I am only marginally cute in a wetsuit. A bit roly-poly. Cute like a penguin. Or an otter. Ugh.

Look at him! There's no chance, lady!

With those hard, prominent knuckles, his hands reach for my hip. I suck in a breath. What. Is. Happening?

Did I... misread his response to my unintentional-but-maybe-a-little-intentional flirting? Oh god. I didn't realize I had this much power. I'd better get that sexual potency of mine under control before... is he coming for my face? What the hell? This hardly seems like a good time to kiss me but... when in Rome?

I lick my lips and lean forward, tilting my head and closing my eyes. I had resolved to say yes to the first attractive guy who seemed to know what he was doing. And Cody's been very kind to me so far, letting me grab on to him when I got spooked by a passing shark or three. Nothing prepares you for sharks. And... he has lips to die for. If we were in high school, I would have written a poem about those lips and found reasons to skulk past his locker like a psycho.

But... oh shit, he's not leaning in to kiss me after all! What?!

Oh Bree, you fool!

I open my eyes as he leans past me, reaching down to grab an oar.

"Oh," I say stupidly. In my mortification, no other words are available but another, "Oh."

And because I'm me, it has taken me this long to remember that I don't know how to read a room. In this instance, the "room" is just Cody. And I'd misinterpreted that signal. All he was trying to do was move me aside to get something.

I don't mean to be selfish; I get up in my head and don't pick up on social cues. Ha. Maybe that has something to do with why I'm still a virgin.

That and the fact that I spend most of my time at my tiny town's library, and the rest of my time playing video games and live-streaming them. I've had one of those gamer channels for a few years now. Let's just say the riff-raff who leave rude comments and send disturbing emails to my inbox is enough to turn me off of men altogether.

Did he see me? Did Cody see me standing here like an idiot with my eyes closed, tilting my head up for a kiss? What was I thinking?

Calm down, Bree. He's just a guy. A standard, considerate, hot, chiseled, fun-loving, go-with-the-flow guy...but do I know him? No! For all I know, he could be one of those turds who leaves garbage comments on my channel.

Crash! Boom!

The sky lights up, and the storm is closing in. My shoulders shiver. This wetsuit is not doing me any favors as I sit out here like a fucking lightning rod.

Yes, says my rational brain. Besides focusing on getting your libido off of Cody, let's focus on the fact that we are in a precarious situation. Be helpful.

Lightning crashes so loud and close that I yip like my mother's annoying Shih-Tzu, and my feet jump five inches off the scratchy turf that lines the bottom of this boat.

I forget the moment of humiliation as terror courses through my veins. Finally, I connect the dots. "Why... why are you getting the oars?"

He smiles that lazy smile like he's unbothered that we could be frizzle-fried out here like a couple of tunas.

"Ah, because the motor won't start." He shoves the smooth wooden handle of the oar into my hands, then crosses to the other side of the boat to fetch the other oar.

"You mean we're rowing? I don't know how. I can't."

Cody nods, then perches himself on the back of the

stern, pushing off of the small floating dock. He lifts his chin and points to the bow. "I'll steer from back here; you sit up there and paddle as fast as you can. I'll talk you through it. You got this, Bree."

I want to ask him to try the motor again. Or if he's sure there's no other landing with shelter nearby that doesn't involve entering a cave. But I don't want to be a whiner. He's a professional. And I have to trust him.

I nod, and I must look scared because his lazy smile transforms into a wide, encouraging grin that reaches his eyes. "I promise, you got this, Bree."

He says my name like a friend who already knows me. I might have grown up on a freshwater lake and learned how to operate a boat, but rowing? No. We are a motorboat community.

Still, I nod, then quickly perch myself on the very tip of the bow. Gulping down my insecurities, I dip my oar into the water and give a big shove.

And we're moving.

I can't believe this is working. I lift my oar and switch it to the other side, repeating the motion. We are pushing this vessel forward. We are going to beat the storm.

Another wild crash of thunder and lightning suffuses everything in white light. Shit.

How close is this storm now? I bite back my fear and just paddle. What's that my dad taught me when I was a kid, and I used to crawl into my parents' bed during thunderstorms? Count the seconds between the thunder and the lightning, and you'll be able to tell how close the storm's center is. I don't know if it's true, but it comforted me as a child. I breathe and start doing that ritual out loud as I paddle. "One Mississippi. Two Mississippi." Crash. Bang! Ugh.

"Almost there! You are doing awesome, Bree!" Cody shouts over the patter of rain hitting the water in fat droplets.

I remind myself that this is the tropics; thunderstorms come and go every day. This will be over soon; maybe we can finish reef diving once. Yeah, that's it.

Crash!

Oh god. Sure, we can finish the dive. If we don't die first.

"Hang on!" cries Cody from the back of the boat. The wind drives rain into my eyes, and a big wave tips us to the side. I reach back and grip one of the grab bars, hugging the oar to my chest and trying not to yelp. And there goes my towel. Oh, no! My beautiful towel. Buster. But no, I have to focus. I'll cry later. Not now.

"Okay, now paddle! Fast!"

I paddle faster, my arms aching from the repetitive motion. Seeing anything with salty spray hitting my face every five seconds is brutal.

Like he said, you can do this, Bree.

I swipe at the water in my eyes and take a hard look ahead. We're approaching the mouth of the cave. In another thirty seconds, we'll be there. Okay, Bree. You have a choice. Either drown, get struck by lightning, or deal with the thing you hate—not knowing what's in that cave. Bats. Bears, snakes, spiders, rodents... whatever else lives in caves. But we're in the South Pacific, so maybe not bears. Jungle cats? Oh god, why is that worse?

Cave it is. Just until the storm passes.

The boat slides into the narrow mouth just as a ten-foot wave crashes over the stern, filling the tunnel with spray and knocking Cody into the water.

I shriek, "Cody!" He's skidded off the stern, his fingers

gripping around the lip of the boat while his body dangles between the hull and the jagged cave wall a few feet away.

He grunts, struggling to pull himself up as the boat jostles violently. Wave after wave sloshes into the cave mouth. He spits out saltwater and roars, "There's an outcropping just up there, to your left. Grab it!"

I look to the left of the bow; I see it. Not enough of anything to tie the boat to, but maybe by holding onto the outcropping, I can pull the vessel farther away from the turbulent waters. His orders fight with my instinct to go to him, grab hold and pull him in.

"I can't! Not while you're just hanging there. Hang on, I'll come get you!"

But the man is twice my size, and there's no way that would work. It's more likely I'll fall in with him.

"Bree! Just do it!"

Right. The outcropping. I rush back to the side, reach out with an unsteady hand and grab the protruding rock and pull, pull, pull the boat forward while simultaneously willing this vessel not to crash into the rocks. Behind me, I hear a loud grunt and a thump and feel the impact of a body hitting the deck. Then I hear the hull scraping against some-thing hard and gritty.

I look over the side, and I see sand. We're in shallow water now, and the boat has beached itself.

Thank god it's not my boat. My dad, a Great Lakes fish-erman, would have a fit over beaching a fiberglass boat this way; there's sure to be some damage to the hull.

I take a deep breath and see Cody jumping to his feet, tousling his hair with two hands and exclaiming.

"Whew! That was fun!" He laughs breathlessly.

Me? I'm shaking, viscerally terrified of small, dark spaces.

Another crack of lightning, just outside the cave mouth, has us both jumping. Cody crosses to the bow, moves past me, and jumps from the boat into the dark beyond.

I yelp.

"Are you okay?" I hear him ask.

I don't answer that because I'm not. Instead, I reply, "It's dark, and there are jagged rocks; how do you know what you're jumping into?"

As my eyes barely adapt to the darkness, I see his tall, tightly muscled outline walking on a ledge of some sort. "Nah. I know this cave better than my own name," he answers.

A hand brushes against mine, and I twitch. "It's just me. Come on. Let's get away from the water until the lightning clears out."

I exit the boat and allow Cody to lead me deeper into the darkness, willing my feet to move with every fiber of will I possess. A lump of panic seizes my throat, and it's hard to breathe. I make a weird, strangled noise, despite all my attempts not to appear like a spoiled baby.

"It's fine," he says, pulling me close to his side. I hear his feet scraping the rock, and then I hear an exhale. A slight tug on my fingers tells me he's sitting on the ledge. "Come on. Sit down and take a breath."

I don't want to grip onto those powerful hands so tightly. The simple touch is making me think about sex. About how he might hold me, pin me down with those hands. Still, I'm terrified of the darkness in this unknown space, so I can't let go of his hands as I gingerly lower myself to the ground.

Cody continues to hold on to me while I hold my breath, half expecting to feel bugs, animals—anything—slither or skitter across my legs and feet. The way he sits and cradles my hands forces me to face him in the dark. I cross my legs and sit on my feet because it makes me feel safe to sit like that. In the darkness, I can see his hair's silhouette, angled cheekbones, and capped, broad shoulders.

"You're okay. We're safe. We'll wait for the storm to pass, and I'll get you back to Little Loggerhead," referring to the tiny island that houses Cerulean Resort & Spa where I'm staying.

I shudder and take a breath. "Is it that obvious I'm afraid of caves?"

Mercifully, he doesn't directly answer that question. "Hang on." He gives my hands a squeeze, and I hear shuffling. He's standing up. "I'll be right back."

I hear his footsteps move to the boat, where we've beached it a good ten yards away. He hops in, and the greenish sky outside lightens his outline as he rifles through some compartments.

When he returns, I ask the obvious question. "Why can't we just hang out in the boat?"

"Eh, some people are afraid of the dark or caves. Some people, like me, are irrationally afraid of lightning. Better to be away from water or anything that could feasibly conduct electricity."

I'm unsure of the science behind that, so I keep my opinions to myself. Besides, he readily opened up about his fears, which endears him to me.

"Here," he mutters, and then a light flicks on, revealing Cody's face and illuminating this small space where we are. He hands me a bottle of water. I unscrew the cap and gulp it down, relieving the salty taste still stinging my mouth.

My eyes adjust further, surveying the small space where we are. The black, glittering rock that we sit on looks like petrified lava. The same craggy darkness shapes our little campsite's rugged walls and ceiling. I peek around warily.

"Don't worry," Cody says, taking the flashlight and showing me all the nooks and crannies from this angle. "No bats in here. The worst thing I've seen is a centipede."

Don't be a baby, Bree. You're in the tropics. You knew there would be bugs. But what I would not give for a bottle of coconut rum and a beach chair right now.

"Oh-okay," I breathe.

"Hey," Cody says, nudging my foot with his. "Let's play a game while we wait out the storm."

The wind roils the sea outside as water sprays in, but not strong enough to reach us where we sit. Another kind of energy crackles over the spot where his toe touched my foot.

"A game? What kind of game?"

With no further introduction, Cody holds up five fingers and launches into Never Have I Ever.

"...Eaten tofu," he says.

"Oh," I say, raising my five fingers, then putting one down. "Ha. I like tofu."

"Blech."

"It's soybeans. You gotta squeeze the water out first."

"Still gross. Your turn."

"Hmm. Alright. Never have I ever gotten expelled from school."

With a snort, he puts down a finger. My mouth drops. "Whoa, really?"

He laughs. "You went straight for the soft underbelly. I was trying to keep the conversation light, Soybeans."

I shrug and say, "You don't have to explain it."

"Long story short," he drawls, his hand going to the back of his neck, "I punched a kid."

I wait, because I want more, but I respectfully move on when nothing more is shared.

"No judgment. Your turn," I say brightly. "Bad boy."

He huffs. "Okay. Never have I ever walked on hot coals."

He puts his finger down, and I don't. "Oh, are you showing off now?" I tease.

"You haven't? You should do it, Beans. There's a guy on Pearl Island who can set that up for you."

"No thanks," I say, even as my body tingles in response to him calling me "Beans."

It's not the sexiest nickname, but him giving me a nickname is pretty cute and sexy.

"Are you secretly the social director of the resort? Trying to squeeze every dime out of me?" I wink, and nudge his leg playfully with my foot.

I could be wrong, but I see a pink hue blooms in the apples of Cody's cheeks. The pink matches the color of those full lips, which turn up at the corner in the first shy smile I've seen from this man. So confident normally. Maybe I should stop flirting. If only my body would get that message.

I hold up four fingers. "Never have I ever given or received a BJ in a movie theater."

Why? Why did that come out of my mouth? I just blurted it out without even thinking. So the libido is running the show. Okay, then.

I keep all four fingers raised. Cody puts down zero fingers.

"Really?"

"What do you mean, really?" Cody huffs with a laugh.

I hope I didn't insult him. "I just am surprised that...

that someone like you has never had that happen to him in a movie theater."

The pink in his cheeks now spreads to his ears, and I watch his broad chest lift and fall with his breathing. I went too far. "Someone like me? Do I look like a guy who would risk getting arrested for public sex acts?"

I immediately realized what I had asked. You see that sort of thing happen in raunchy comedies, but there are significant consequences in real life.

"Wow. I do not know what I'm talking about in the arena of sex. I feel like such a dope for asking that."

"Don't," he says. "We didn't set any ground rules for these questions. If someone wanted to be intimate with me, we'd be in private. I don't want to share my woman with anyone."

My pussy clenches in response to the words, "my woman."

I don't like anyone implying they own a woman, but the way he says it makes me wish I was his. Get real, Bree. You're getting too deep now.

And before I can stop my rambling mouth, I blurt, "I've never made out with anyone, so I don't even know why I ask these questions."

He blinks. "How old are you?"

My hands sweat. "Twenty-eight."

His Adam's apple bobs, and he's looking at me with an expression I can't identify. Repulsed fascination? Very possible. Behold, the lone 20-something virgin of the islands. Step right up and buy a ticket, folks.

With a raspy baritone, Cody pivots. "Moving right along. Ah... okay... thinking...."

Crap. I made him uncomfortable at the mere mention

of making out. He's put off at the idea, or maybe just by the idea of making out with me.

"Got one." Cody holds up three fingers. "Never have I ever had a breakfast date." He puts one finger down, and so do I.

I sigh. "Does brunch count?"

"It counts."

That's three fingers left for me, two for Cody. "That was actually the last date I was on. I met up with a fellow gamer online who thought he was nice. Turns out he spent the whole time staring at our server. Too bad because breakfast is my favorite, and he ruined my whole day."

Cody clears his throat. "Sorry that happened. Me, I just enjoy cooking breakfast, and I'm more of a morning person. So... yeah, I like to cook breakfast for my dates."

The implication of that makes me a little nauseous. "Oh," I mutter. "You mean like the morning after...."

He shakes his head. "No, no. Well, occasionally but only with past girlfriends. I don't sleep around if that's what you think."

I clarify, "That doesn't matter to me. Just because I'm a virgin doesn't mean I expect everyone else to be."

I realize what I've said like a complete idiot when Cody's eyes widen.

"Ah, shit. I said that out loud, didn't I?"

He swallows again, and I see him trying to train his face. "There's nothing wrong with that. After the last question, I assumed that was the case."

"Sure, there's nothing wrong with it," I say with a snort. "It's just an endless topic of conversation among my friends."

Cody's eyebrows narrow at me. "Why? It's none of their business."

I shrug. "It wouldn't be if I hadn't been clear I wanted to lose my virginity on this trip."

If someone dropped a pin, it would echo endlessly through this cave.

I am pleading, begging Mother Nature to open up the rock floor and swallow me. Why? Why do I say these things?

A crack of lightning startles me, and I hope that's enough to change the subject.

"Storm's getting farther away now," Cody says.

I look out through the cave mouth and see the formerly green sky has turned dark gray, and the rain is going at a diagonal rather than a straight line. He's right.

"Never have I ever... been arrested," I offer.

We both put one finger down.

"Beans!" Cody guffaws with a surprised laugh. "I thought you were a good girl."

"I am! At my cousin's house on the Saint Mary's River, I was being stupid. I... I didn't know the international border was right down the middle. I thought the border was land! One day I was swimming, and I just kept swimming, and the next thing I knew, the border patrol was after me. Did you know the border patrol has boats?"

I tell the whole gruesome story of detainment, clad in nothing but a swimsuit while border guards stared me down, having to call my aunt to meet me with my purse so I could show ID. "It's the worst thing I've ever done."

By the time I'm finished, Cody is gripping his side like he has a stitch from laughing so hard. "Oh, Beans. That's tragic."

I can't help but laugh at myself, no matter how many times I tell that story.

"What about you? Share, please."

"Alright. You don't officially know this, but I got arrested for buying beer for someone underage."

"Cody!" I say with an exaggerated gasp.

He covers his eyes in shame. "I know! It was an accident, kind of. It was my brother's graduation party from college. He had invited his roommates. One of those guys, who I didn't know that well, was only 20, and he asked me to pick up some beer, and he would pay for it. Someone saw me putting it into his trunk of the car he was driving, then alerted the cashier, who called the cops. Let's just say I almost ruined my brother's grad party. I'm not proud. It was stupid that I didn't even ask him how old he was."

I can't disagree. "It wasn't the brightest move, no. Has your brother forgiven you?"

"Sure."

"Then you should stop beating yourself up."

He pauses for a few seconds, then kicks at some rocks with his water shoes, resting his elbows on his knees. "You're right."

"I know I am."

He chuckles. "I like you, Beans."

Heat begins at my toes and takes off through my body, making my scalp tingle.

"Your turn. You've got one finger left, and I have two."

Cody gasps, then grabs one of my hands and examines it comically. "My god, what happened?"

He makes me laugh, which doesn't slow down my racing pulse. The mere touch makes me lusty, and I have no reason to expect I have a shot. The man looks like a sculpted cover model for Men's Health.

No way he's a valid candidate.

"Simmer down, class clown. Your turn," I remind him, still laughing and gently pulling my hand back.

His deep-thinking hum does dark and sultry things to my body, vibrating below my waist. This once-comfy wet suit now feels rough, constricting, and... in the way.

I nudge him again, playfully. "Don't think; just blurt the first thing that pops into your head."

"Here we go. Never have I ever slept in anyone's basement."

I put a finger down, and he doesn't. We're tied at one remaining finger each. I eye him skeptically. "Do they not have basements where you're from?"

He nods. "They do. But basements freak me out. Anytime I was invited to sleepovers as a kid, and it turned out to be a basement thing, I'd make up an excuse for my mom to come get me."

The image of a smaller version of Cody, curled up in a dark living room at midnight, watching out the window for his mom, is so sweet, sad, and cute that I can't help but make the most sympathetic noise. "Aww. Poor widdle Cody."

The man scrubs his face with one palm. "I don't know why I told you that."

"You picked it. And don't be ashamed; it makes you seem more human and less Greek god of the sea."

He gives a tortured laugh. "Poseidon?"

I cringe. "Forget I said that."

He speaks slowly and tells me, "I don't think that's possible."

Pressing the meat of my palms into my eye sockets, I will away the memory of what I just said.

Cody shifts on his bottom and pretzels his legs together, so we're sitting knees to knees. I drop my hands from my face and look. His skin there is rough with decades-old scars. I reach out and touch one knee.

"You have a lot of these."

He shrugs. "Childhood misadventures. I was a little too fearless about some things, too fearful about others."

He's so warm. The warmest thing in this dank, eerie cave.

"How are you not afraid of caves but scared of basements?"

"Oh. That," Cody continues. "Because when I was five years old, my idiot stepbrother was obsessed with Freddie Krueger and hogged the remote," he explains.

I hold up my hand. "Say no more. I hate horror movies."

"Same," he replies. "I like scary movies. But gory? No thanks."

I gasp. "Will you marry me?"

Without hesitation, he says, "Absolutely. Let's go right now."

I'm laughing, but he's not. And I'm down to one finger, and he's still got two. How did I, a virgin who's never been kissed, come so close to losing this game?

My turn. Possibly my last question, so I'd better make this one count. The amount of things we've revealed to each other feels... unbalanced.

"Never have I ever slow danced with a man."

Neither of us lowers a finger.

"Wait, you haven't?" Cody asks.

I shake my head from side to side. "Nope. In middle school, I slow danced with a boy at our first school dance. But never a grown man."

He looks like he has a follow-up question but bites his lip to keep that question from bursting out of him.

"If you ask it, I will answer it," I urge.

Cody makes a noise between a grunt and a hum like he's thinking better of it.

And then, he surprises me with: "My turn. Never have I ever kissed anyone on a first date."

He puts down his last finger, and I still have two remaining.

That one was a gimme. "I already told you I never made out with anyone. Are you just trying to make fun of my lack of experience?"

He gives me a heated look. "No."

I roll my eyes, not ready to hear whatever story he has to tell about kissing on the first date. "Let's have it, then. Who did you kiss?"

That easy smile spreads across his face, crinkling the corners of his eyes. He shows me those beautiful teeth. This boy hit the jackpot in the good genes department. So unfair.

He blows out a breath and finally says, "You."

For one long moment, we hold each other's gazes.

"Unless you have a time machine or can see into the future, we didn't date, and we certainly didn't kiss."

He winks. "The day is still young."

"Confident much?" I say with a chuckle, even though my insides tremble with need.

"Not at all," he answers. "Just optimistic."

I smile. "You're out of fingers," I rasp. "What do I win?"

"Hmmm," Cody hums, looking up at the cave ceiling and rubbing the scruff of his chin. "Bragging rights. And the winner is honored to share some snacks your friends packed for you."

Of course. I'm starving, and he must be too. "Absolutely, have at it!"

Minutes later, we're stuffing our faces with sandwiches. Then, I find the genuine treasure at the bottom of Laura's mini cooler. I carefully open the cellophane wrapper and inhale the sugary cinnamon scent.

"Is that an oatmeal cream sandwich?" Cody asks.

"Yes, my favorite!" I exclaim.

He laughs. "I haven't seen one of those since my last trip to the big island."

There are two in there, so I chuck the other into his lap.

"There goes my keto. Worth it."

I stare at him. "Oh god, you're keto?"

"Keto, CrossFit. Total nightmare."

My eyes bug out. "Do you hate yourself?"

He winks, bites into the snack, and then lets a pornographic moan. "Shit, it really is worth it."

"I never noticed a CrossFit gym at the resort," I point out, taking the last bite of the sweet, cinnamon goodness.

"There's not one," Cody replies. "Couple of buddies and I do it on the rainforest trails. We take guests out there, too. You should sign up."

I sit up straight and give an exaggerated tut-tut. "Are you saying I need to work on my body?"

"Oh god. No. No, no, no. I would never say that. You might have fun, that's what I meant. I wouldn't change anything about your body. It's perfect. It's ridiculously perfect...."

Now he's overcompensating for saying the wrong thing. "I was kidding! Let's not get carried away." I look like an Oompa Loompa in this wetsuit that doesn't hide a single curve or flaw. I'm okay with that.

"The truth is, I used to run a CrossFit class. That's over. Today's my last day, so you're lucky. I won't be bugging you to sign up."

I blink at him. "It's your last day?"

He nods again. "I put in ten years. Time to move on."

Whoa.

"Ten years? I feel bad you're spending your last day like

this. You should be slacking off with your work friends. Not hanging out with a stick-in-the-mud."

His eyes flick from the top of my head to my lips. "Now I know you're lying to yourself. You're not a stick in the mud. I figured that out when you tried to kiss me on the boat."

I sit straight up, my jaw dropping. "Excuse me?"

Cody lifts one shoulder and grins crookedly. "You're quite the thrill-seeker."

"Ugh!"

"I'm not saying it would be a bad way to leave this world."

I am so embarrassed. "You noticed that?"

"Sorta tough to miss it when a beautiful woman licks her lips in my direction."

"Oh, my god." I cover my beet-red face.

"Relax, Beans."

I whine, but it's muffled by my hands. "No. I'm never going to relax again."

There's a pause, and I see his expression has grown serious when I peek through my fingers. "Maybe there's something we can do to help with that."

"Huh? Help with what?" I blurt when I feel his hand against mine. Specifically, his fingers cuffing each of my wrists and slowly, gently, moving my hands away from my overheated face.

Looking directly at him again, I notice how his lips are parted, his eyelids hooded. He angles his face and leans in.

"To help you relax."

"Oh," I say dumbly.

Cody stops a few inches away, softly grinning. I blink and lick my lips. When his gaze flicks down to spot my tongue doing that, Cody's nostrils flare, and his grip on my wrist tightens.

I lean in, and our lips meet for the first time.

Electricity—the fun, sexy, not deadly kind—flows up and down my spine as his soft, full lips sweep over mine. Again and again, tenderly, playfully.

I take it up a notch by opening my lips and brushing the tip of my tongue against his bottom lip.

The sound of our kissing causes my nipples to feel tight, and this wetsuit is becoming increasingly uncomfortable.

He doesn't take long plunging his tongue into my mouth to taste me.

Heat and wetness pool within my core. Cody changes the angle of his face and kisses me more deeply.

Cody pulls away from the kiss just far enough that I can feel his breath whisper across my skin.

"Would you consider accepting my help with your little...problem?"

TWO

Cody

BREE BLINKS at me slowly as a smile brightens across her face.

"Yes."

My favorite word.

She characterizes herself as a stick in the mud or a shrinking violet, but that's all wrong. She's the introvert who hangs with extroverts.

When I'd met her and her friends on the dock this morning, her friends were loud and gregarious.

"Here are some snacks and drinks. We know how hungry you get," said the blonde one with the high-pitched voice.

The taller, dark-skinned one with the braids had brought a first-aid kit that was even bigger than the one I keep in the boat. "Here," she had said, handing over the box with the big red cross on it. "She's obsessed with stingrays, jellies, and shit. Keep an eye on her, please."

"Yes, ma'am," I'd replied, nodding and stealing a glance at the quieter, shorter woman with freckled, peachy skin, dark curls, and a cover-up that fell to her ankles. She'd been clutching a towel with a dog on it, plus a well-worn paperback.

Here, in this cave, she's just herself.

"Where should we do it? My apartment? Your room at the resort?"

Bree shrugs. "Why not here?"

I look around skeptically. "Because we're in a dirty cave? Because there's no bed?"

She takes in what I've said and is thoughtful for a second. "I always said I wanted my first time to be memorable. And I don't want my friends to know it's happening."

I know exactly what she means.

"You deserve a bed, though."

She nods. "I do. But..." Her eyes dart to the mouth of the cave. The rain is slowing down, but the waters are still choppy. "Who knows when I'm just going to be ready to do it again? And...not to be crass, but... my friends packed extra towels."

So practical. I might love this woman.

Too bad I fly back to the States tomorrow, and I don't even know where she's from.

"Whatever the location, you deserve more ambiance and comfort. And romance."

"I was told there was nothing romantic about anyone's first time," she says, dropping her head and looking up at me shyly.

My hand automatically reaches up to cup her cheek. "Then let me disprove that theory for you."

Bree's eyes flash, and she pulls her bottom lip into her mouth.

"I'm going to be bad at this; just going to warn you now."

"Inexperienced does not equal bad," I assure her.

Bree's shoulders drop slightly.

She's still wearing her wetsuit, her body is tense, and she won't stop talking.

"Sh-should I get naked now?" Bree asks.

"Not if you're not ready," I tell her, stroking the length of her cheekbone with my thumb.

"I am ready. Put me in, Coach."

"I don't mean mentally. I mean..."

I lean in and draw her face to mine, feathering my lips over hers. "This is what I mean."

My body responds to the slight noise she makes with this first teasing kiss. My cock goes rigid, and I want to touch her everywhere.

I need to get us out of these wetsuits, but I need her desperate first.

THREE

Bree

CODY TOWERS OVER ME, cupping my cheek and stroking my face as he kisses me.

The first kiss was so careful, testing me out, seeing if I was ready. Oh god, am I. I'm so ready that I can't control this silly urge to moan.

The noises I make must be okay because the next thing I know, Cody delivers more prolonged, wetter kisses that send curls of heat down to my sex. He pulls away briefly with a short, playful nip to my bottom lip.

He's being careful with me while my body is screaming for more. I knew those lips would be great at kissing. I didn't realize how freaking wet he would make me with a first kiss.

My emotions are all over the place, and I can't stifle a giggle when he stares down at me, checking on me.

"Did I do something funny?" Cody asks, his expression bemused.

My cheeks heat, and I blurt out the truth. "My vagina is making a slip-and-slide inside this outfit."

Cody huffs out a laugh. "Oh, my god; I love you."

When my eyes widen, he winces. "I shouldn't have said that."

At the same time, he runs his thumb across my dampened, swollen bottom lip. He's not that sorry he said that. And neither am I.

Love isn't necessarily roses and engagement rings and wedding bells and forever. It's possible to love someone for just one week or one day and let them float out of your life. Lovable people come and go, and we remember them fondly. I don't stop caring about them.

"Don't sweat it," I say. "I've made an idiot of myself on this excursion enough times to cover up ten accidental 'I love yous.'"

He says nothing but continues stroking his thumb across my bottom lip. Follow your instincts, Bree. You're in a cave, you know. Where humankind used to live and fuck and fight off predators. Now's the time to give in to the primal urges.

Following that instinct, I close my lips around Cody's thumb, wetting it with my tongue, swirling and licking slowly. His already hooded eyes grow narrow with lust. A growl sounds deep in his chest.

This man tastes like saltwater and smells like the outdoors, and I want more of him. My greedy mouth pulls his thumb in deeper, then slides it out like a popsicle.

"Fuck," he whispers. "You're so damn sexy, do you know that?"

I don't know if he wants me to answer that. I continue sucking and licking, sighing noisily. I've heard women's sexy moans before, but what I'm doing sounds weird and needy.

Messy and whiny like a little girl, and I can't help feeling embarrassed. I should have watched more porn to practice for this moment. Cody is doing A-plus work. I should do more, shouldn't I?

My better self, the part that knows better, snaps into place. Stop thinking of it like a group project, it says. He likes you. He wants to have sex with you. If he doesn't like it? Fine. You never have to see him again. Go with the flow and don't think of it as work. Do what you feel.

I feel like getting on my knees, freeing that hog between his legs, and going to town on him.

I aim to do just that as my hand slides down to cup that oversized package at the front of his wetsuit. Oh... wow. It's big. And long.

Another groan slides out of him at this touch. I like this. A lot. I stroke my thumb up and down the hard length, pressing and squeezing, noticing the ridge at the head.

Cody sucks his breath in through his teeth. "Beans. Wait. Shit, that's good. But no... wait."

He withdraws his thumb from my mouth.

"W-wait?" I gasp, both of us ignoring the bit of drool that also spills from my mouth.

"The touching... and watching you suck my thumb like that gonna make me come too soon."

I've pushed him too far, too fast.

Cody's expression is kind, though. He wraps both my hands in his long, strong fingers.

Slowly, he raises my hands to his mouth and lazily presses a soft kiss to each tip. Each fingertip, each knuckle, watching me melt. At the end of this seductive ritual, he softly bites at the meaty spot below the base of my thumb. I suck in a breath at the scrape of his teeth. Does he not know what that does to me?

With a lick to the spot where he bit me, I feel a needful throb at my core. He repeats this on my other hand, biting a little harder. I gasp and press my teeth into my bottom lip. God, that feels crazy good. He again licks a tiny red spot where he bit me, then comes for my face.

Before our lips meet again, he murmurs, "That's my bottom lip to bite. Gimme."

And oh my god, he bites so deliciously. Not too hard, not too soft, but enough to make me wonder how I'm not passing out from dehydration and lack of blood to my brain. Because all the moisture in my body? Is slicking my pussy.

My voice turns husky without me trying. "Cody. Please."

The man growls and captures my body in his steady arms, crushing me against him while his mouth owns me. Claims me.

"My baby doesn't need to beg."

My heart flutters, and my sex clamps down hard at the sound of Cody calling me "baby." I have to remind myself it's a temporary pet name. It's a sex thing. He's in the heat of the moment.

With a firm tug from one of his index fingers to the zipper, my wetsuit falls open down to my waist. He helps me wriggle free of the sleeves, then tugs it down to my ankles so I can kick it away.

I'm now wearing nothing but my two-piece swimsuit, and his eyes roam everywhere over my curves, my pouchy belly, and my thighs. I feel naked already, even though he's seen this before.

I'm determined to stop overthinking and follow his lead. So when he tells me to take off my swimsuit, I just do it. I tug the top section off and shimmy out of the bottoms.

I don't know what I expect Cody to do next, but it's not to stand there in complete awe.

"You're gorgeous, Bree. Look at you."

I peek down at my boobs and blush. They're not bad. I blink at him shyly and notice his chest's rapid rise and fall. I also see he's still wearing his wetsuit, but oddly, that doesn't bother me.

"Beautiful," he repeats, closing in and cupping one breast in his big hand. He swipes his index over the nipple, and I gasp again at the sudden rush of sensitivity.

A minute ago, I cared about sounding too appreciative, too much like a wanton, needy girl. But I don't care about that anymore. I like how it feels when he touches me, cupping one breast in each hand and thumbing my nipples so delicately that they tighten instantly under his touch.

Lava churns inside my veins. My core is soaked, gripping nothing and crying out to be filled. Still, his caresses and playful teasing heighten my need second by second. Cody is driving me so insane that I have to give myself over to the moment and close my eyes.

The sensation of his wet mouth suctioning around my nipple makes me want to dig my nails into his skin. Is that normal? I don't know what to do with my hands, but tangling my fingers into his short, damp locks seems like the thing to do. I scrape my fingertips through the silky smoothness and suddenly wonder what his other hand is up to.

That's when I feel those fingers travel down, stopping to grip the flesh along my hip.

He growls on my nipple, scraping his teeth over the sensitive peak, then pops it out of his mouth to blow on it. I'm quivering as I press my body harder against his mouth, needing more. My arms circle around his neck. Oh, yes. I like this better, my hands out of the way.

"I've wanted to grab onto these hips since I first saw you swimming under the water. I didn't know they would feel this good in my hand. Next time I take you, it's gonna be in a bed, and I'm gonna grab on so tight and push in so damn hard."

I moan at his words, arching my back. Even though he doesn't mean it, I don't want him to stop saying those sultry things. "Cody," I half whisper, half whimper, my body begging him to keep kissing, keep up the pressure.

He seizes my breast again, hungrily taking in more.

"Bree. Will you let me make you come with my fingers?"

I'd rather have the D, but I'm desperate for anything and everything.

"Mmm-hmm," I hum in agreement, nodding my head enthusiastically, unable to form words.

He cups the back of my neck, then fists my hair, dragging me into his intoxicating kiss. He licks the seam of my lips, and I open to him, letting him lick inside slowly, wickedly. The hand on my hip roams over my lower belly, and I tense up.

He pulls away from the kiss to hold my gaze while he palms the front of my pussy, that small triangle of short, curly fuzz. The nerves under the skin there erupt in delight at his touch.

I'm lost in the dual sensation of his hand exploring my sex and his mouth ravaging mine.

My legs spread to let him in, heart pounding as Cody's teasing hand finds its way to my folds, caressing the outermost areas of my lips at first. So lightly, I might go insane. His lips, hands, and mind are so playful and teasing, working me up into a needy, demanding frenzy.

"Oh!" I cry when his fingers nudge apart my lips and

slide into my wetness. One finger finds my aching hole and slips in, massaging the sensitive walls. He works me over, and it's so good, but not enough.

"Cody."

A second finger joins the first, stroking inside, exploring, creating slippery noises that, before today, I never would have considered a turn-on. Oh, but now, I'm losing myself in all of it. The dragging in and out provokes my body to act on its own, jerking against his hand.

Need. More.

I'm almost falling apart when Cody adds the third finger. He stretches me, and my senses erupt at the fullness... but still, it's not full enough.

It's like my body knows what to do, attempting to ride those fingers, suck them in and spit them.

His breath is hot against my neck. "Good girl. And you said you'd be bad at this. Look at you."

He kisses me hard, as if he's known this is what I wanted all along. I moan into his mouth, pressing against his body while I ride him, grinding against his hand. But I can't get a stable hold enough to relieve my aching clit.

As if reading my mind, Cody slows the stretching, in-and-out motion and finds the tiny, throbbing nub at the front of my cleft.

"Here? This what you want?"

He's teasing. He knows.

I whimper, "yes, please," my eyes rolling back in my head. I am a bundle of nerves—a moaning, sighing, gasping heap of jelly whose sole focus is making more direct contact with that thumb circling my clit.

It's so good I'm barely aware of my nails pressing into the bunched muscles of his back.

Finally, the circling ceases, and he grazes that button. It only takes that one light touch before I explode.

"Ohmygod. Ohmygod!"

In the past, I have made myself come many times. I've shouted, laughed, cried, and even hooted. But never all at the same time. The sound that comes from my smiling mouth is a choked, incoherent sob.

Cody speaks orders into my ear, softly. "I got you, Beans. Hold on."

My eyes flutter open. "Huh? Oh. Yes, sir." I don't know why I called him sir. It just fell out. I do as he says, holding on tight as he picks me up and carries me.

The light becomes brighter as we approach the mouth of the cave, and sunlight streaks in and reveals a blue sky and semi-calm waters outside.

Is it time to head back to Little Loggerhead? Nah.

He sets me down gently on my feet, and I watch him strip off the wetsuit and his Speedo all in one go. Well, then.

The cave makes strange shadows, at least until he stands upright, flinging off the leg of his wetsuit. And then I see it. Thick at the root, surrounded by short curls. His cock is deep pink, veiny and long, curving slightly in the middle as it stands straight up. The tip is somewhat darker and glistens with moisture.

I watch Cody fist that long shaft and squeeze, dragging his hand from the root to the tip. On the outside, I'm calm, but the cat in heat on the inside is ready to scratch if he doesn't let me have my new toy.

My new toy? God, what's wrong with me?

Nothing. Nothing's wrong with me. This is fun. So much goddamn fun I might need to pinch myself.

"You see what you've done to me, baby? I'm so hard I could pound nails with this thing."

"Please don't," I say, trying not to laugh. Okay, now I feel better about my weird thoughts. "Pound me instead. I think that's how you use that tool."

He lets out a growly laugh that stirs up that familiar feeling in my sex again. "Shit, you got a sexy mouth on you, Beans." A wave of hunger washes over me from watching this man pump himself up and down. Those sinewy forearms ripple with the movements of his tight grip. I'm aching again. Throbbing. Needing.

"I got a mouth that's hungry for more kisses, if you got any," I answer back. God, I'm such a dork. I don't know how to talk dirty, but he's making me feel adequate about my attempts.

I watch him step into the beached boat. Curiously, he goes to a small compartment behind the steering wheel and pulls out a tiny metallic square pouch. I can't believe I'm staring at this man slowly unrolling a condom over his cock. It feels so invasive to watch this, but he smirks when he catches me.

I could ask why he even had that on hand, but I'm too fucking relieved he had a stash on board. I don't need to know why.

He looks around curiously. "Where's that towel, the one with the dog?"

I nip this in the bud before we ruin the mood. "Lost at sea, don't worry about it."

He takes a beat and studies me.

"Sorry."

I shake my head. "Forget it. It's fine. Where were we? Oh. I think..." I go to my wet beach bag and find a couple of towels that are only halfway soaked. He takes them from me, spreads the dry ones on the boat's seat cushions, sits down, and beckons me to come aboard.

I don't know how I expected the first time to go, or what kind of position it would be. Face to face, straddling him, wasn't the first thought in my nasty head, but I love it when Cody pulls me onto his lap. I feel so safe. I love it when he adjusts his erection so it nestles in my folds, the thick base pressing against my clit.

Wow. Double wow.

I don't understand why, but this makes me feel powerful. Automatically, I rock my hips forward, reveling in how his face tightens, his jaw clenches, and his eyes turn to slits as he stares up at me.

"Fuck," he seethes. "Bree."

Imagine my confusion when he plants his firm hands on my hips to still me, stopping this delicious friction we both need.

"Wait, Beans. Hold on."

I want to claw him. And he wants to wait. For what?

I study his face. "Cody?" I swallow hard.

He looks like a man who just got hold of his senses.

And I'm on the precipice of being humiliated. Devastated. Mortified. And strung alone an outrageous amount.

FOUR

Cody

"BREE," I breathe. "Just hold on a minute."

I want to memorize this moment and hold it in my heart for the rest of my life: Bree straddling my lap, her face the picture of lust, her lips bee-stung from our kissing, her cheeks and chest flushed pink. Not to mention her breasts, level with my mouth, glistening with my spit. Behind the wild, lustful look in her eyes, her dilated pupils, my Bree contains universes that I haven't yet explored.

I know that this isn't over after today. I know we're meant to be together. It may seem insane. But I believe in soul mates, and I know she's mine.

It's not just our bodies that are made for each other, nor the way our bodies move together, so wildly in sync. Her playfulness, sweetness, sense of adventure, and kindness have a stranglehold on my heart, and I don't want her to let me go.

"Cody?"

The look in her eyes is fearful. I've just been sitting here, staring at her, taking her all in with my eyes, imprinting her on my mind. Meanwhile, she's there, wondering what's wrong with me.

"I'm memorizing you."

Bree cocks her head. "Memorizing...me?"

I nod. "Because I never want to forget this moment."

An emotion surfaces on her face that I can't identify. She exhales like a great weight has been lifted.

"I was so worried you'd changed your mind," Bree explains.

I lift my hips, with her still seated there. "Does it feel like I've changed my mind?"

She lets out a yelp of surprise at being lifted, then falls against my chest. "Ha, no. It doesn't."

I angle forward, nuzzling my face between her breasts.

Bree's hands go to my hair. I love the feel of her fingers there, petting me like a good boy.

Again I take one of her nipples into my mouth and then the other, playing and enjoying how pink they are from my relentless mouth, my scruff. My hands roam over her hips and her ass. Every curve fits in my grip. When my fingers glide over the split of her rump, she rises higher onto her knees, forcing her tit to pop out of my mouth. With my nose, I nuzzle the undersides of her sweet melons, kissing and tasting the skin over her ribcage and tummy.

My fingers curve inward at her split, drawing out a whine from my Bree.

"Ungh," she moans, her head lolling backward. I know how she feels. Her body, curves, spirit, and every inch of her have devastated me.

With one hand fixed to her ass, my other hand reaches around and notches the tip of my cock into her passage.

"Good?"

She nods and bites her lip. "M-more."

I smile, lowering her down more, inch by inch, stretching her, watching her face for any hint of pain.

I may have stretched her to fit me, but she's still so fucking tight. So tight that my whole body ignites with an overwhelming urge to cram it in fast. I grit my teeth and stay still, waiting on her.

Another inch. At one point, she winces, and I stop. "Want me to wait?"

She smiles, and I feel her muscles relax, letting me in deeper. "Don't you dare," she rasps, lowering herself until she's fully seated.

I simply breathe. "Bree."

I harbor a tiny fear that I'm too much for her. That I'm making all of this a bigger deal than it needs to be. But I'm not a one-and-done kind of guy. I won't be getting over her. Ever.

When I say her name, "Bree," again and again, I feel the heated grip of her sex.

She says my name back to me, her voice brittle and raspy, my cock twitching inside her.

Her eyes widen as I grow harder, thicker, and hotter with every passing moment.

Slowly, I help her grind, guiding her speed, savoring the feel of her tight cunt pumping up and down on my shaft.

My eyes rake over her, then land on the unbelievable sight of the joining of our bodies. The image of her soft pussy dripping her juice all down my cock, smearing my balls, leaving her scent on me, makes me ready to explode.

Gradually, using my grip on her hips, I teach my Bree exactly how I like it. A little faster. A little rougher, if she can handle it.

She's already so tight that I'm groaning in the pain and pleasure of it. But I need more.

"Baby, can you flex for me? There. Oh shit. Shit, shit, shit. Good girl...oh my god."

I lose myself in her—in her juicy cunt, sun-kissed skin, swollen lips, pineapple-scented hair. Everything I taste and smell and feel is Bree. I don't know whether it's so good it hurts to hold in my cum, or it hurts so much to hold in my cum that it's good.

I'm determined to keep it together and let her have her way. Let her play. Bree grinds hard, thrusting her pelvis against mine, and I understand.

"That naughty clit need another spanking?"

She gasps and then exhales a laugh. "Such a weirdo."

"You love it," I tease.

I watch her throat bob. "I do."

As she whines, I scoot her back just an inch, just enough to make room for my thumb, to give her some relief.

Her drenched, stretched pussy continues to milk me, squeeze me, destroy me while my thumb strums her overheated button.

Without warning, her body tenses, her lips part, and her back arches into me. Her climax wrecks me, her passage spasming so damn hard.

"I'm gonna come, baby."

At the word "baby," Bree's body bears down on my cock again, flexing so fucking hard that my release barrels into me like a freight train. Everything goes black for half a second; I'm only aware of Bree's arms wrapped around me and her whispers against my neck.

"Cody. Cody. Holy shit, Cody."

"Bree, you're fucking fantastic."

We breathe as one as we wetly kiss each other through our quivering tail end of our mutual release.

My lips act on their own, needing to kiss her fiercely everywhere: her cheeks, her nose, her throat, her forehead, her temples, her ears, that tender skin under her earlobes. There's no part of her I don't want to taste.

"Bree. Tell me your last name."

Bree lifts her head from where it rests on my shoulder and blinks at me.

"Weathers. Why?"

"Because," I answer, "I'm going to look you up when I go back to the States."

I can't read her expression.

So, I hold my breath and wait for her to say something.

FIVE

Bree

DID he just say he wants to see me again?

"You mean, like, for a booty call? I don't even know where to begin with that."

Cody's eyebrows knit together again with that serious look. "No, Bree. I don't do booty calls."

My brain takes a moment to absorb this.

I don't speak for a long while as we peel away from each other, and he helps me tidy myself up with the towels. He takes such good care of me, just like I knew he would.

I could get used to this. But I shouldn't, because he's leaving. And I'm nothing more than a resort guest he shouldn't be fucking.

We silently don our swimsuits again and together—carefully—lift and shove the boat back into the water.

Using the oars, we work together to push the boat out of the cave mouth. Cody tries the motor once we're in deep enough water and away from the reef.

I crouch off the bow and sit on the cushions, hugging my knees into my chest. With two pulls, the motor starts up, and I stare at the cave mouth. I feel the thunk of the throttle, and he turns her nose away from our little island. I wave at it. "Bye, Virgin Sacrifice Cave."

Cody snorts.

"Virgin Sacrifice Cave."

I shrug, and he chuckles.

He adds, "You know, I meant what I said. About coming to see you."

My gut clenches. I know there's no way Cody will come all the way out to where I live. It took an act of Congress just to coordinate this trip with my college friends from a city only five hours away.

"I'm from a tiny town in the upper peninsula of Michigan. Where are you from?" I ask.

Cody squints as if the horizon holds the answer to that. "I haven't really been from anywhere in ten years. West Virginia is where I grew up. I'm headed there tomorrow. A buddy of mine is a rafting guide, and he has a small apartment above his shop that I can use while I'm helping him out for the season. It's not much, but it's something."

I blink at him. "Why are you leaving, then?"

I worry that my question is offensive, but he takes it in stride. He shrugs and shifts the boat to a higher speed. "I've never had a plan. When I applied for a job at Cerulean, I didn't have a backup plan. The Pearl Crescent Islands are enough of a draw that if you land a job here, you simply take it. It's literally the most lush, beautiful spot on earth. On top of that, the resort's parent company is Rushmore, and nothing beats those benefits."

Oh yes, I've heard about that. Not that know a thing about the mysterious billionaire Rushmore. But I chose to stay at his resort based on the common knowledge that he treats his employees well.

"But, ten years is enough. I want to go back to the States and start something new, even if I don't know what that new start is."

West Virginia is far, too far to have any claim on this man. There's no way this will work. Cody is a dreamer. While that's endearing, it's not practical.

"So it's not your dream to be a river guide?"

He answers, "I'll always want to be near the water. I just don't know in what capacity. I'm keeping an open mind. What about you? I don't even know what you do for a living, Bree Weathers, from some mysterious tiny town."

When he winks, it sends a pleasant shiver down my spine, remembering how he touched me minutes ago.

"It's called Cedar Isle. It's a little place on the remote edges of Lake Huron. I run the library. It's not huge, but we can get anything anybody needs. And not just books! Through the interlibrary loan throughout the state, we can get kitchen appliances, lawn and garden tools, you name it."

"Wow, that's so cool."

"It's a nice thing to have for a remote place. It's pretty cold and lonely in the winter. A lot of snow. In the summer we get a good number of tourists. There's a marina, the best ice cream in the world, and we have a school where you can learn to build wooden boats."

Cody lifts an eyebrow. "Wooden boats, eh?"

I nod. "Like the old Chris-Crafts that hardly anybody makes anymore. It's kinda famous. The whole place is pretty charming and right on the water. You'd like it."

Why did I say that? He has no intention of seeing me again, and the sooner I face this fact, the better.

"Of course, I would. You live there."

Even after everything we did, he can still make my cheeks heat with words like this. I have to tear my eyes away from him and stare at the sunset.

He asks, "Do you like it there?"

"I do. It's not as sophisticated as my girlfriends' life in Chicago, but it suits me. We have Les Cheneaux Islands. Kayaking, off-roading. Whatever you want. The water is not like this, though; it's cold. Lots of shrinkage; you'd hate it."

Cody laughs, and we carry on this conversation about our lives until we return to the dock, where a group of people about our age are waiting around.

"Cody! Where have you been?" one of them calls out.

I hope that nobody can read it on our faces.

Cody hops out of the boat, then reaches back to hold my hand as I hop out.

"We got caught in the lightning storm. We had to shelter over by the reef. It was wild."

I'm just standing here awkwardly, ensuring I haven't forgotten anything, pretending there's nothing more to that story.

One of the men hands Cody a beer. "Well, you're a free man now. We better hurry up and get you drunk, so we can send you home with a proper hangover tomorrow."

Deep breath. This is it.

This moment becomes doubly heartbreaking when I recognize the bush pilot, Austin, who flew me from the big island to Little Loggerhead earlier this week. Tucked under his arm is the hot blonde from the photo that I remember seeing taped to the plane's instrument panel. She looks content, gorgeous—and pregnant. I try to swallow the knot in my throat. What if I followed Cody on his rambling adventures? What if I got pregnant? I already know he'd be a great dad.

Wait, where are all these feelings coming from? He punched my vee card and that's that.

Right. Another deep breath.

I paste on a bright smile. "Well, bye. And thanks for the dive. It was great," I say, squeezing his arm in a friendly gesture. My words are barely audible over the din of all his friends.

"Wait. Bree."

I roll up on my toes and hug his neck. "It was so much fun. Come say goodbye in the morning before your plane takes off, okay?"

Why did I say that? I don't want to wait to say goodbye in the morning. We're doing this now.

I try to pull away from the hug. But he's not letting me. In my ear, he murmurs, "Come hang out with us tonight. Please. You met Austin on the plane, right? Come hang with his fiancee, Sierra. I think you two would hit it off."

I slide out of his arms and look around at this group. They seem fun, but they're also loud and keen on getting Cody totally hammered. One of them, a tanned woman with sun-bleached hair, hooks her arm through Cody's, even as he still hugs me with his other arm. "Come on. You promised before you left that I could see your break-dance moves."

On the one hand, I want to punch her in the nose. She's got that certain "one-of-the-guys" vibe that some women have that I can't stand. And I don't like that about myself. I'm quiet when I'm in large groups, and she's super outgoing and fun and probably has a favorite shark. She's the type who looks incredible in a wetsuit. She's likely super friendly, and therefore I hate her.

Ugh. I need to grow up and get out of here. Now.

I wriggle free of him and raise my hand in a goodbye

salute, smiling bravely. "Have a good night. I'm going to meet my friends; they're probably worried about me."

I leave, not knowing if I will ever see him again.

I know he'd be nice to me if I stayed. But it would take away his last moments with people he's known for ten years, which wouldn't be fair. Even if one is a hot blonde surfer chick, who looks like a supermodel without a stitch of makeup.

I scurry back up to my room at the hotel, chuck my wetsuit, swimsuit, and towels into the laundry bag, and head for the shower.

I accomplished what I set out to do, and that's that. Done and dusted.

After showering, I find my girlfriends, Violet and Laura, drinking margaritas by the beachside pool.

Behind them, the sun is setting on the Pacific.

"How was snorkeling?" Violet asks, squeezing me to her side when I sidle up to her barstool. Her brown eyes study me intently.

"Great," I say. "Amazing, actually. The storm cut us short, though. We're lucky we didn't get struck by lightning."

Laura gestures to Violet. "That's right, it was super windy just as we left the shopping center, and then started pouring buckets while we were inside the restaurant for lunch."

"I'm glad you're okay," Violet says, still eyeing me. Can she tell? No, there's no way.

"So, did you guys buy me anything?" I ask.

Violet laughs. Laura nods, opens her straw handbag, reaches in, and hands me a small box. "From both of us." She smiles, stretching the gently sunburned pink skin of her cheeks.

I open it to find a delicate gold chain with a gold pendant shaped like a stingray.

"It's beautiful! You guys, oh my god!"

"It's to commemorate your first time," Violet says.

"What? Oh. You mean my first time snorkeling."

Both Violet and Laura look at me like I've lost my marbles. "Yeah," Laura says slowly. "Because you always said stingrays were your favorite. Ever since we watched Finding Nemo."

Violet chuckles. "Of course, our nerdy Bree's takeaway from that movie was an affinity for the teacher."

"I'm not a teacher," I remind her. "I read to toddlers during story hours and do crafts with upper elementary kids on weekends. But I'm not a teacher."

To be fair, though, I could barely describe what my friends do for a living. Violet is the vice president of marketing for something having to do with food at sports complexes. Laura works for the mayor's office. Writing... speeches? No idea. Their job titles are so long, and I don't get it. Me? I'm a librarian. That's it.

"You should come work for me," Violet says. "I mean if we're going to talk about work."

I shrug and take a sip of her margarita. "Nah. I like where I am."

Laura looks at me quizzically. "You like living in a town with only one tiny grocery store and two stoplights?"

I correct her. "We have two flashing lights, one grocery store, and two convenience stores, thank you very much."

Laura winces, and Violet groans as if that would be the worst thing in the world.

"So, what's on the agenda for tomorrow, ladies?"

Laura shrugs. "I dunno. We're just going to put one foot in front of the other and see where the day takes us," she says, sucking down her margarita and gesturing to the passing waiter for another one.

See where the day takes me. I wish I could be more like that. Cody's like that.

Maybe I should be more like that. That will be the key to moving on from... losing my favorite towel that captured my favorite memory with Buster. The world's best dog who crossed the rainbow bridge years ago. That's it. That's what I'm sad about.

But I'll be okay.

Whatever happens, I'll be okay. Won't I?

SIX

Cody

LITTLE LOGGERHEAD ISLAND may be small and peaceful, but the nightlife is wild, and you never know who you'll run into.

On this night, the music is loud, the drinks are flowing, and the dance floors are so crowded with sweaty, sunburned guests that it's difficult to find any one particular person.

Finally, I spot Bree's friends at table at the beachside bar, about twenty yards away. They look like they're wrapping things up for the night, so I start heading that way in a hurry.

My beeline gets interrupted by a severe looking guy in a black suit definitely not intended to blend in to the beach nightlife scene. He nudges me off the boardwalk. I should be intimidated, but this resort plays hosts to so many VIPs that I'm used to guys like him. Also, I'm on a mission.

"I'm walking here," I snarl.

"Correction: the royals of Austero are walking here," he says in an accent I don't recognize.

He steps in front of me as a glamorous looking couple walks by, waving at onlookers.

"Who the hell is that?" I ask of no one in particular.

Someone nearby guffaws, "That's Princess Angelica and her American husband."

I could not be less impressed by foreign royalty, so I'm not waiting. Instead, I take the scenic route to the bar through the dense landscaping. That's a no-no for us employees, but I'm over it.

Finally, I reach Bree's friends just as they're getting up from their table, sloppily slinging their purses over their shoulders and cackling about something.

Where's Bree?"

I try to sound casual, but I know what I look like as I pick palm fronds and other foliage off my shirt.

One friend of Bree, who introduced herself as Laura, informs me, "She said she had too much sun today and went to lie down. Wait. Why am I telling you this? Who are you? I'm sorry, she had too many margaritas. Or maybe that was me. Anyway..."

The one called Violet waves her arms in the air and then gently bear hugs her friend from behind. "Silly, this is the dunky hiving instructor. I mean the... hiccup... the hunky diving instructor. What she's trying to say is we've all probably had enough sun and booze today, but Bree is the only one of us who knows when to call it a night. What's your name again?"

"Cody," I say, tilting my chin down. "If you see her, could you tell her I need to talk to her?"

I don't think there's any universe where these women

would tell me Bree's room number. I'd be more disturbed if they blurted that out to me in their drunken state.

I'm thinking of my next step when Violet smirks. "Why? What do you need to talk to her about? She didn't hit you up to be a candidate, did she?"

Both girls laugh. And my stomach drops. I can't let them know the truth.

"I... I don't know what that means, but no. I just... I wanted to tell her that she... she won a drawing."

"A drawing?" Laura reaches for another cocktail, but Violet wisely shoves a glass of water into her hand.

"Yeah. All guests who do an expedition are entered into a drawing for a free outing, and she won! So, let her know if she wants to go, meet me at the airstrip tomorrow at nine a.m."

Violet eyeballs me, and then her eyes flick to the shopping bags in my hands. She isn't buying it. And I don't blame her. "The airstrip? Don't you mean the dock?"

"Oh, yeah. No. The airstrip. It's a secret spot on the other side of the island that most resort guests don't get to see."

Laura coos. "Oooh, that sounds fun!"

Violet squints. "Secret spot, huh? Hmm. Well, we're about done here. You can come with us and tell her yourself!"

These bags are heavy, and I want to give Bree her presents. I ditched my going away party early; I hate long, drawn-out drunken goodbyes. They'll see me off in the morning before I go to the airstrip. I'll make sure to knock extra loud on everyone's doors.

FIVE MINUTES LATER, Violet, Laura, and I are at the door of their suite.

Laura calls out, "Bree! Honey, wake up! We're home! The chunky diver who looks like Adam Driver wants to talk to you. Hey, that rhymes." She cracks herself up while Violet hisses and fidgets with her keycard.

"He does not look like Adam Driver."

Someone put me out of my misery.

Laura snorts and tee-hees. "I told you everyone looks like a Star Wars character when I'm drunk. It's a special type of beer goggles."

Someone, god, Yoda, anybody up there, please get me out of this hallway. Please.

An answer to my prayer comes in the form of my absolute angel rounding the corner of the hallway. She's not in her room; she's walking the halls...in tiny pajamas? I don't like that, but thank god she's here.

Bree's eyes narrow on me, and she looks from me to Violet to Laura, then back to me.

"Uh...what the fuck is going on?"

And...my angel is pissed.

SEVEN

Bree

I WISH I'd never left my room on a fruitless search for vending machine snacks. Now I'm hungry and unable to sleep.

Grumpy, I head back upstairs to my room.

And now, what's this I see in front of me? Cody, standing outside of our suite, holding up a drunk Laura, whose hands are all over him.

Well, shit.

I'm not prepared to see him like this, and my green-eyed monster emerges. "What the fuck is going on?"

"Bree," he says. "This isn't what it looks like."

Be cool, Bree. Be the breezy girl. The fun girl. The easy-going girl. The "just one of the guys" girls.

I swallow. "It's fine."

I paste a smile onto my face and slide past my friends to open the door.

"Bree," Cody presses. His voice sounds worried. Well, he can worry all he wants.

Laura pipes up as I push the door open. "I'm so glad we found your diving instructor. He walked us back to the room because Violet's pretty drunk; I don't know if you noticed that."

Violet rolls her eyes as the three of us file inside.

Don't look back at Cody standing in the hallway like a lost puppy. Don't do it, Bree.

"Wait. Bree. I need to talk to you."

I pause, my hand on the door. Without turning around, I ask, "Did I forget something in the boat?"

"No, I need to talk to you."

Violet turns to me. "You going to let him come in? He seems eager to talk to you. Maybe he's here to help you with you're little... problem?"

"Vi."

"Okay, okay," Violet relents. "I'll butt out. But don't worry. If he tries anything, just say the word. He might be big, but we can take him down amongst the three of us."

Violet gestures at Cody, implying that she's watching him.

I let him in and point to the couch in the suite's main room. "Wait here. I need to talk to my friends."

He comes in with his haul of shopping bags, sets the bags on the sofa, and then perches himself on the cushioned arm.

Once I'm alone with my friends in Violet's room, I tell them everything.

EIGHT

Cody

I'LL WAIT HERE all night if I have to. If she tells me to leave, fine. I'll go.

A notification sound comes through on my phone, and I'm grateful for something to pass the time.

Wayne: "Let me know if you're still interested in the apartment upstairs."

Hmm.

I need to think. I swipe up and fart around on the browser for a while.

Well, look at that. Did I just google the boat-building school that Bree mentioned?

Yes. Yes, I did.

The tuition is not cheap, but I have money saved. And I could save more money if I moved there as a permanent resident first... am I downloading an application right now and requesting an interview?

Yes, I am.

Me to Wayne: "I'll need the apartment for a couple of weeks until I figure out what I'm doing."

Wayne: "Cool. I can pay you weekly if you want to help with our river trips."

Me: "Perfect. If things go as planned, I think... no, I know... I'll be going to Michigan after that."

Wayne: "For work?"

Me: "Met a lake girl. I think I want to learn how to build wooden boats."

Wayne: "Sweet. See you soon."

Wayne is one of those friends who doesn't pry with many questions and accepts things as they come. I have a feeling if I stayed and worked at the outfitter for the next ten years or ten days, he'd be chill either way. Still, I won't leave him high and dry without a river guide at peak vacation time.

The door to Violet's room opens, and Bree steps out.

I make room for her on the sofa, but she walks right past me, crosses the room, and opens another door.

"Come on, then, let's talk."

I follow her, close the door behind me, and lock it.

Bree lifts her eyebrows at the noise of the lock and sits on the bed.

"Bree. I swear I wasn't trying to go home with your friends. They invited me up to see you, so I went with them. Also, I wanted to make sure they got back to their rooms safe—"

Bree holds up a hand and cuts me off with a small smile. "I know. They explained it. I believe them. And I believe you." She swallows, then eyes the bags I've set on the floor beside her bed. "So, what's this about? I thought we were all set for me to stop by the airstrip tomorrow to say a friendly goodbye?"

I scrub my palm over my face. Can she not see what's happening? Does she really not feel the connection? "Bree. I want you in my life."

A pause follows. She pulls her lips into her mouth, thinking about how to respond to this lunatic in front of her.

"You'll be in my life. I'll always think fondly of you, Cody. We had so much fun."

That's it. I'm laying it all out there, and Bree can either reject me or agree to give this a shot.

I come to my knees on the floor in front of her and take her hands in my hands. "Beans. We've only known each other for one day, but I need you in my life. Every day. I want to kiss your bad breath mouth every morning, eat breakfast with you, and have adventures with you every day. Give me a chance to be your guy. Tell me you don't have time for a boyfriend in your tiny little town, and I'll leave you alone."

She looks at me as if to say, what am I going to do with this man? "One fuck in a boat does not equal a successful couple. It's not enough to uproot your life."

I squeeze her hands and say, "I have nothing to uproot. I have zero roots. If I ever wanted roots, I'd put them wherever you are. I want my roots to be all mixed up with your roots."

"Stop saying root."

"Okay."

Laughter breaks the tension, but her face gets that serious look again. "I can't let you move for me."

"If it doesn't work, I'll figure out the next step. All I'm asking is for a first step. Just one."

I need to stop talking and let her think. Bree bites her lip some more and rubs her chest. "What's in the bags?"

"I brought you some snacks... and...."

"Say less, I'm starving... oh my god, you got oatmeal cream sandwiches! How?"

"I called around, and one of the vending machines in the other hotel had some." I let my hand drop to her knee and squeeze. This is a lie, of course. I went to the big island and ran some errands after I ditched the party. I would move heaven and earth to please her.

"And... sour cream and onion chips! Yay. And... what is this?"

She's already digging through the second bag, and I hold my breath.

"Is this... a beach towel?"

I say nothing and wait.

She peers inside, then stops and looks down at me. "Cody, what did you do?"

I lift one shoulder. "Nothing." The truth? I bribed the kid at the drugstore photo lab. They say those photo gift things take a week but do not.

Her hand goes back to her chest, and her eyes well up. Maybe this was a mistake.

"What did you do to get this photo?"

Uh... now is the part where I tell her I might have found the same photo on her Instagram account, screen-grabbed it, and sent it to the photo lab. I just say it like it's as simple as making a phone call. Creepy? Absolutely.

"You what?" Her voice is watery as she unfolds the fluffy towel on the bed gingerly as if handling a bomb.

"Buster," she sobs.

Shit. I'm an asshole. This was too far. I crossed the line trying to do something extra nice.

"I'll take it back."

Through tears, she shouts, "The fuck you will!"

The next thing I know, her arms are around me, and I'm

holding her, comforting her while she lets it all out. "Thank you," she murmurs into my shoulder, soaking my tee shirt.

"You're welcome," I say, confused, barely able to speak above a whisper around the knot in my throat.

"That is the weirdest, nicest thing anyone has ever done for me...for no reason!"

I reach up and pet her hair, comforting her. "It's not for no reason. I did it because you're incredible, and I'm nuts about you. And I'm leaving tomorrow, and I don't want to. I wanted to give you back something you lost. It's not enough to represent my feelings, but it's a start."

She sniffles and buries her head into my shoulder, hyperventilating into my collarbone.

If I wasn't such a perv, this would not give me a hard-on right now. But I can't help it around Bree. She's touching me. Breathing on me. That's enough. She could slap me, and that would make me stiff.

I press my hands into her back muscles, working them up and down, up and down, until her crying stops.

With one deep breath and a tired exhale, she lets go and smiles up at me.

"I guess I really miss Buster."

Oh, my god. I didn't even realize that Buster was... oh shit.

"You have nothing to be sorry about, Bree. I'm sorry for... I don't know. Being overwhelming."

She shakes her head and wipes her nose. "You're not overwhelming. I'm just shocked."

"It was too much."

She sighs and dabs her tears with the back of her hand.

I can't help myself; I lean in and kiss each remaining tear away.

"If you weren't you, I'd say that was a stalker move."

I smirk. "Maybe I am a bit of a stalker because I'm coming to Michigan."

She makes a derisive noise. "Yeah. Right."

"Wait and see."

Bree blows out a breath and thinks for a minute. Then her gaze slides up from her lap, over to my hands, up my body, and finally lands on my face.

"How about one more time for the road, stalker?"

I'm now more confused until she pats the bed next to her. "Now that we have a mattress?" she adds with a smirk.

Oh. Shit.

"But I made you cry...."

"Seriously, are you going to sit there and tell me you got all this, did all this for me, and didn't anticipate me crying?"

My mouth opens to answer "No," but she tells me not to answer that.

"Just kiss me before I start crying again."

Bree's lips are soft and warm. And her breath is minty, with no traces of the salty kisses we shared. Hotter and hungrier, too.

My tongue slicks into her mouth the second she gives me an opening. She gives me one of her signature whimpers, trying not to show how turned on she is.

That's fine. If this goes where I think it's going, I'm gonna make her scream.

My hand cradles her head while I gently lower her onto her back. Lying down and kissing her on the mattress feels different from messing around in the cave. Of course it does.

Her small hands fist my shirt, our teeth clack together, and our tongues surge into each other's mouths.

I shouldn't be doing this without a verbal commitment from her that she'll give me a chance. But if my Beans wants the D, she's gonna get it from no one but me.

Bree pushes me away and breathes, "What time is your flight again?"

"Nine-thirty a.m."

"Too early. Not enough time."

She fists my shirt again and pulls me down on top of her, slicking her warm, wet tongue into my mouth. The fingers of her other hand scrape through my hair and rake down my neck, shoulder, and arm until our fingers braid together so tight it hurts.

She's right. There's not enough time. Not enough time to savor this body, this whole woman, in the hours we have left. Maybe I can ask Austin to delay picking me up on the dock. He's a good dude, he'd understand.

But I know that's not how it works. If Austin's little island-hopper plane is late to the big island, I miss my connecting flight to the States.

"Beans, slow down and let me make love to you."

Her chest heaving, she rasps, "I was thinking instead, maybe you could show me all the positions you know."

"That's... an efficient use of our time," I laugh.

She nods. "First fuck me doggy style. Then I thought maybe we could do the reverse cowgirl thing... then...."

I waste no time while she's listing off all the things she wants to do, my hand cupping the warm juncture of her thighs and my face nuzzling and rubbing her tits through the fabric of her pajamas while she continues to chatter.

"Hmm. A-and then, you tie me down... oh... right there... ah... if we can find something to tie me down with and tell me I'm a good girl while you... mmm... pound me until the bed breaks."

I laugh while I brush my hands over her breasts, thumbing her nipples and dragging a firm knuckle over her heat. "Ungh," she moans. I'm amused at this enthusiasm, even as my cock hears all this and roars at me to set it free from the confines of these khaki shorts.

"Holy shit, Bree. Is it Christmas already?"

"I'm serious," she says, her leg reaching around my hips to grip me closer.

I kiss that saucy mouth again, then deliver long, wet kisses down her neck, across her collarbone, and over her breasts. My mouth nuzzles and plays with her soft, pillowy tits, my desire for her spiking as her nipples tighten under my touch. "I'm not a fan of you waltzing around the hotel with no bra on," I mutter, nipping her skin through the soft material.

"Hmmm. Then you'll probably be extremely chagrined to learn that I didn't wear any underwear for my midnight waltz, either."

A low growl escapes me, and I rock my hips against her side. I go to investigate with one hand first.

Roughly, I slide my hand under the hem of those shorts and notice the familiar, soft curves that perfectly fill out my grip. I squeeze hard, and she hisses, then sighs.

"You like it when I squeeze you tight, Beans?"

"Mmmhmmm," she hums, licking her lips.

"How 'bout this?" My hand roams deeper, four fingers sweeping into the cleft between her cheeks.

Bree purrs, biting her lip, her leg hooking me tighter.

"And this?" I say, letting go and then lightly slapping that fleshy cheek.

She gasps, her eyes widening, lips parting in a sexy half smile. "Do that again. Spank me harder."

I obey and spank her harder, ensuring my slap lands only on the fattest bit of her bottom. That jiggle is so hot; I wish I had a better view of it.

"That's for walking around with no undies in a hotel for anyone to notice you."

Her eyes narrow, and she smiles, letting go of my shirt. Bree's hand wanders to her chest, where she idly caresses her sweet melon while looking thoughtfully up at the ceiling as if she's just remembering something. My jaw clenches when she remarks, "Now that you say that, there was a group of soccer players downstairs who smiled and said something to me, but I didn't understand the language."

My nostrils flare. "Bree. That's not funny." I say this even as my cock twitches and grows harder.

She pouts. "Sorry. I meant football. We're not in America, are we?"

"Bree."

"Hmm. I wish I knew what they said. But I heard a whistle. That's nice, right?"

I know she's playing, but my reptile brain is freaking the fuck out.

I don't like this game. I don't like how tight my shorts feel while she fucks with me or how goddamn pained I am waiting to tear that pussy up.

With one swift move, I have her flat on her stomach so I can spank the other cheek.

Her voice cracks with her moans as she begs me to do it again.

Her shorts have ridden up, and her bottom is pink. My dick throbs at the sight of it.

What is happening?

I'm not like this. I've never done this before, and I'm questioning everything I know about myself. With each spank to that round bottom, her moans threaten to bring me to my knees.

Now seems like a good time to let her writhe on the bed; it'll give me a minute to get rid of these clothes. So little time left, and I want as much skin-to-skin contact as possible.

I chuck my shorts and underwear across the room and tug off my shirt. Bree lifts her hips and does the same, tossing aside her pajamas. I'd already seen most of this earlier today, but this moment hits different. Showing up at her door in the hotel, having sex in a place where I worked until today, somehow feels dirtier. She's as tempting as sin, and I'm built for taking that fruit.

The only thing stopping my eyes from staring at this radiant beauty before me is the sense that I'm being watched. It's weird. Then, looking down at the mattress, old Buster's eyes judge me.

I know, dude. But she begged me.

I fold up the towel and place it reverently on the side table.

When I return to the bed, I pull the waiting wanton woman on top of my chest. My hands get lost in her hair, and my mouth finds its home against her lips.

"I fucking love your kiss; I could kiss you forever, Bree."

"I love kissing you, Cody. Every time I close my eyes, I feel your lips on me."

That...gives me a good idea.

"Bree, I need to taste you. Can I? Please?"

"Mm. I love it when you say please." Bree nuzzles our noses together and kisses me again before lying on the pillows and spreading her legs for me.

I could kiss her everywhere, all night long, but there's only one place I'm craving right now.

"Oh my god," she whimpers when I kiss and taste her outer lips. "Oh my god, oh my god."

Her hips thrust into me, begging for more. My thumbs

spread open her pussy lips and reveal her dripping softness, her juice flowing just for me. I should go slow. I want to go slow, but I'm a greedy son of a bitch when it comes to Bree.

Licking from the back to her clit, her sweet essence coats my face and tongue. I suck and swallow down all her sweetness, owning this pussy. Owning my Bree.

I flatten my tongue and give a hard sweep over her clit, which sends her bucking against me. I do one more sweep and then dive my tongue into her hole.

Her gasps, her trembles, tell me she's close. I anchor her knees over my shoulders as I continue devouring her relentlessly.

My mouth owns her clit again, sucking and nudging the tiny throbbing button.

Bree's thighs squeeze against the sides of my head; her voice is hoarse when she cries out her orgasm, my mouth ravenous for her pussy.

"Cody... Fuck, fuck, fuck... Fuck!"

I never thought my Bree could curse like a sailor. My Beans is full of surprises.

NINE

Bree

I AM A RAG DOLL. A happy, satisfied rag doll.

But Cody's not finished with me. After he finishes slipping on a condom, he flips me over and tells me to get on all fours. But my knees have already turned to jelly. This man is determined to lay waste to me. And, isn't that what I asked for?

I pant from the climax he tore out of me with his evil tongue.

"I can't. I want to. I can't... my knees. I'm still shaking."

This large, muscled man lowers his body on top of me, covering me with his weight from my shoulders down to my feet. Shoving my hair out of the way, Cody sloppily kisses up and down the back of my neck.

Against my neck, he murmurs, "Remember when you didn't think you could paddle? And you didn't think you could help me beach the boat in the cave, but you did it anyway?"

"Uh-huh."

"So do it anyway. I want to watch my dick slide into your pussy from behind and pound that sweet peach."

Oh. My. God. Yes, please.

"O-okay," I say weakly.

He peels his body off me, helps me steady myself on my knees, and then knocks open my thighs.

"Good girl. Now get on your elbows and arch your back."

He whispers all the praise with my rump as high in the air as I can manage. And then slides that fat dick into my folds, using me to lube himself up.

I look at him over my shoulder, his lips still swollen from our kissing. He looks down again, and something changes on his face, making his jaw tight.

"What's wrong, Cody?"

His words tumble out in an almost incoherent rattle. I can tell he feels shaken, but it takes me a minute to figure it out.

"Did I hurt you? Why didn't you tell me to stop? Your poor little butt, it's all pink; I see a handprint... fuck... I don't know what I'm doing, do I?"

My breath catches. "Oh... Cody, it's fine. It doesn't hurt."

I insist he did nothing wrong, but he doesn't hear me. The sting of it, the wildness of it, and everything that followed made me happy. "I liked it."

"I have to make my baby feel better," he says with a growl.

Who am I to complain about this beautiful man with sexy lips feathering gentle kisses all over both cheeks? The soft kisses to my rump turn me on in a whole other way, and

I soon forget about my tired legs, my spent pussy, the sweat dripping from my brow.

Instead, I rest my head on my forearms and close my eyes. And enjoy.

The man says he's crazy about me. Crazy enough to follow me home, and I'm not even scared of that. Maybe I should be? But I'm just not.

His kisses roam lower, to the spot where my bottom meets my thigh. I let out a long sigh, feeling like a spoiled kitten.

The soft touches between my thighs and his lips on my body relax me into a state of bliss, while also working me up into a level of confounding arousal. My skin is hot. Instead of feeling empty of thoughts, I'm clear. Powerful. Sexy. Beautiful.

I look back at Cody and watch him slide his cock in. The way his eyes roll back in his head is too much.

"Fuck... Bree..." Cody almost sounds like he's laughing, but I understand what he's feeling. I'm there, too. We're both overwhelmed.

When he looks back down, he blurts, "Look at you. Just look at how wet you are."

I wish I could, but I swear to god, if he takes a photo, I will slap him into next month. But I know he wouldn't ever do that.

Cody grabs my hips then, and the slow slide in and out quickly speeds up. He's using his hands to steady us, pull me back against him, and fuck me deeper and harder.

I squeeze down until I hear the telltale curse. He felt that. And he loves it.

I keep squeezing as he pushes, pulls, pounds and digs his fingers into my hips. The pinch is so good, but the slamming of that cock is even better. My ears make a memory of this: the sounds of wet skin slapping, his grunts with every thrust, my uncontrollable moans, and whimpers.

I could keep going like this forever.

His pounding speeds up, and my hands scrabble at the top edge of the mattress. The sheets are a mess. Without warning, he lets go of my hips and angles his body over mine, his dripping wet chest heaving against my back, his hands in my hair.

On the next surge of his cock, I feel the tip of that monster hit me in an entirely new way, somewhere deep inside my passage. I come apart with a scream as a wild rush of pleasure pushes me over the edge...nearly knocking my head against the headboard.

"Shit, shit, shit, shit, yes. Fuck, yes!" Cody roars. The curses continue to tumble out as that hard cock pumps out his release. My body and mind explode in overstimulation as I keep pushing back. I keep moving, milking his cock, making it spit out every drop. I wish he was spilling it inside me. He is mine, and I want all of it.

I don't know what will happen tomorrow or next week, but I know this man is mine. All mine.

All the things he's been trying to tell me. All the nice things he did. How he took such good care of me when I was scared in the cave. How he pushed me to do what I thought I couldn't do.

He deserves a chance. I deserve to be honest about my feelings. I don't want to walk away from this.

Exhausted, spent, and too weak to think, the two of us tumble to the mattress in a pile of intertwined arms and legs. Our breath is one breath, our body heat is the same, and the taste in my mouth could be him or me. I don't care. It's just... us.

I think I must have drifted off to sleep for a few minutes

because when I wake up, Cody is cleaning me up with a warm, wet hotel towel.

When he finishes with that and comes back to bed, I open my eyes to see Cody's small, earnest smile.

The look on his face grips my heart.

That's the face of a man in love.

He slowly traces his fingertip over my bottom lip, then over my top lip, and says, "You have perfect lips, did you know that?"

"No," I breathe.

"Shame," he says. "Because they are unendingly kissable."

"I don't want you to go," I blurt.

His brows knit together, and he sighs. "I don't want to go either."

"Stay. Stay with me in this hotel room for the rest of the week. Cancel your flight and stay with me."

Cody chews on his lip.

Is he actually considering it?

TEN

Cody

I KNOW it takes a lot for her to say this. And I desperately want to stay.

"Thing is, I promised my buddy. But I'll be in Cedar Isle as soon as the summer's over."

She closes her eyes and bites her lip.

"Bree. I'll be there."

"I know you will. I just... if we're going to give this a try, then let's get started."

"Beans, it'll fly by before you know it. Promise. And listen. You made this trip to be with your girlfriends, didn't you?"

She nods.

"Then you should spend this week with your friends. And I'll see you in less than two months."

She nods, then blinks at me slowly.

"I don't think I can come to the airstrip. I don't want to cry in front of your friends."

I sigh, and I understand. I don't want her to do anything she doesn't want to do.

We share one more long, aching kiss until the very last second that I have to grab my things and head to West Virginia.

ELEVEN

Bree

IT'S the end of July, and I'm wrapping up the Summer Reading Program with a visit from a park ranger who has brought in a range of local wildlife from the rehabilitation center. Owls with bum legs, an eagle rescued from an illegal zoo.

It's the most excitement I've seen at my little library all summer. I look around the room at all the familiar faces, the moms and dads who visit our little library and keep it afloat by checking out the same books for years. They don't know how much I appreciate them.

They also can't see how utterly sad I am on the inside.

Sad and unsure.

I blink several times while trying to pay attention to the park ranger. I almost miss the tall figure engulfing the entire space of the small vestibule of the building's entryway.

That familiar shape steps out of the shadows and into the room, sharp eyes on me.

Cody.

A knot forms in my throat because I knew this would happen; I just didn't know when.

I certainly didn't expect it to be this soon.

I stand up and cover my mouth. He approaches me with a lazy swagger and a smile that matches it. He drops his backpack to the floor. "Hey, Beans."

Embarrassingly, I flap my hands like a bird because I'm surprised and emotional.

"I thought you weren't coming until the end of the summer!"

"Meh. I cut out early. I wanted to surprise you. Besides, I have to report to orientation tomorrow."

"Orientation?"

He nods. "Some hot chick I know told me there's a school for making wooden boats around here somewhere."

He nods, and I let out a yip. "Cody, I'm so excited for you!"

"Only thing... I can save money if I have a permanent residence here. It's a little last-minute on my part, but do you think you could help me find a place?"

I jump up and down, seeing all the pairs of eyes watching us intently instead of Ranger Steve. Then, I pull my guy into my closet-sized office and shut the door.

"You're staying with me!"

"I am?"

"Don't be stupid; yes, of course, you're staying with me."

"I don't want to be a freeloader."

I pinch his arm.

"Ouch," he says, laughing and rubbing the red spot.

"There's literally nowhere else for you to stay. I would challenge you to look around, but you won't find a place unless you want to drive from Sault Ste. Marie or Saint Ignace, both too far away. Or Mackinaw City, but no fucking way my boyfriend will live south of the bridge; I'm not paying tolls to visit you. You're staying with me."

The whole time I'm sputtering all of this, Cody is cupping my face in both hands, and that familiar touch that I've missed—his thumb drifting up the line of my cheekbones—squeezes my heart.

"I love you, Beans."

Finally, I can say it. "I love you too, Cody."

We kiss, laugh, and kiss some more, and a tear falls down my cheek.

I'm so damn happy.

He did what he said. I knew he would. I knew it in my head, but my heart was still unsure.

Now that my head and heart are in alignment, finally, I'm excited and proud of myself for putting one foot in front of the other.

EPILOGUE

Five years later

CODY

THIS IS my fifth summer with Bree. My fifth year in this tiny Lake Huron town. It's been three years since I graduated from boat building school and two years since I got a job managing the marina.

Bree continues to work at the library. And our two littlest beans—Coral and Pearl—are getting ready to start kindergarten at the elementary school.

I'm getting used to the winters. I don't mind the cold so much. My only complaint is the constant rebuilding projects at the marina. Every time the waters rise, we wake up to pieces of the dock floating away. It's expensive, but the hardened locals are used to it.

Today, I've just finished repairing one of the boat slips,

and although I'm bone tired, I still go to work in my wood-shed. I have a surprise for my wife.

Sauntering through our neighbor Grace's patch of beach on my way home from work, I find her setting up her fire pit. I've helped her and her family fix their dock and repaired their boats half a dozen times over the last five years, and in return, they've been great neighbors, always ready with a beer and a chair by the fire.

She nods a friendly hello, and I ask her, "Do you think you could check on the girls tonight, say around nine? I have a surprise for Bree."

We work out the details, and she promises that she, her daughter, and grandson will peek in on the kiddos.

Back in my workshop, I put the final touches on my project. Bree is not home with the girls yet, probably on a play date with friends.

When I finish, I open the shed doors, back my trailer up to the concrete, and load up my surprise. Carefully, because I'm the only lunatic on the lake who does this sort of thing on his own, I haul it to the nearby boat launch and drop it into the water. Then, I steer our shiny new boat to the dock in front of our house.

The girls come home just as I hop out onto the creaky old dock.

Keeping everyone from heading out back to the dock is a game of fakery and persuasion, but I somehow manage.

After dinner, we put the girls to bed by reading Sleeping Beauty to them for the hundredth time. It's not my favorite story, but the girls love it, so who am I to argue?

Now that they're five, I still can't believe how cute they are. They both look like their mom, with freckles and curly brown hair.

"Daddy, sing the song," begs Coral, who still holds my hand when I put her to bed. I hope she never stops.

Pearl has already kissed her mom and me and is out like a light.

Coral is the temperamental one. But I wouldn't want her to change, not for the world.

I sing the song terribly, and Coral's asleep before I finish.

Carefully, quietly, we sneak out of the room.

But instead of leading my wife to bed to watch a movie until we're sure the kids are asleep before some quiet frisky time, I show her outside the back door.

"Where are we going?" Bree asks.

I grip her hand in mine and lead her down to the dock. Fortunately, the sun sets so late here that she can still see what I've got waiting for her in the water.

The finish on the wood gleams in the setting sunlight.

Bree presses our joined hands to her cheek. "What did you do? Did you steal a boat from the school?"

"Nah, babe. I made it."

She gasps. "I knew you were working on something!"

She screeches all the way down the dock. Her excitement does not stop until we're on our way to our date night spot.

"Wait! Oh my god, the kids! Are you nuts?"

I shrug lazily. "Edna's gonna check on them."

"When she's halfway through a bottle of red?" Bree snorts.

"I'll text another neighbor, then. But she won't let anything happen to them."

"You're right. I trust you. Where are we going?"

I smirk. "Funnily enough, I found this cave in the islands. I thought we could check it out."

"Cody. No, you did not."

She's right. I tried. No such luck.

I drop anchor in a scenic spot in the middle of the cove, near the sandbar where Bree used to spend the day with her family. It does my heart good to know I can give those same sorts of memories to Coral and Pearl and whoever else might come along.

I'm tired from working all day with my hands, followed by hours in the workshop, but I'm never too tired for a date night with my wife. After we devour all the oatmeal cream sandwiches and chips I brought, we take turns giving each other foot massages.

"Nothing says I love you like snacks and a foot massage," Bree chuckles. "Just don't think about touching my lady bits after you've been touching my feet."

For five years, this woman has made me belly laugh every day.

"I would never do that to you, not in this boat, anyway," I say, scooting in closer and pulling her onto my lap. "It's too nice."

We laugh and kiss, and with the distant sound of laughter, chatter, and dogs barking echoing off the water, it's the perfect magical moment.

"You wouldn't? How disappointing," Bree says with a pout.

"Nah. A boat this sexy, you don't need to use your hands."

Bree hums in pleasure. My mouth finds its way down her throat, lower, lower, and lower still until I'm home.

Amidst her cries, she finds the wherewithal to tell me what she really thinks.

Bree sighs. "I really know how to bring home the best vacation souvenirs."

I kiss her on the nose, and she kisses me on my cheek.

"As long as I don't end up in your yard sale."

She laughs, then kisses and bites my neck. "Never," she croons. "Unless you try to sign me up for CrossFit. Then all bets are off."

I kiss the patch of skin above the vee in her shirt and nuzzle against her chest.

"Deal."

THE END

THANK *you for reading V-Card Vacation! If you enjoyed this little story, please consider leaving a review.*

Want to know more about Sierra and Austin? Read Babymoon next.

Want some sweet summer vacation stories from Bree's neck of the woods? Try the Paradise Lane collection:

Gretchen and Matthew in Off-Season Stud

Josh and Penny in Midsummer Fling

Cash and Caroline in Are You For Reel?

Curious about Princess Angelica and her American husband? Read Shipped.

For more of the multi-author Filthy Dirty Summer series collaboration, check out the complete set, available on Amazon.

MORE BY ABBY KNOX

All Abby's books are stand-alone romances, each with its own HEA. No cliffhangers or cheating!

Abby's latest releases:

Filthy Chef

(workplace romance/one-night-stand-turned HEA)

Reckless Royals

Favored Prince (royal family/American bride)

Bad Prince (forced marriage/divorce pact)

Wild Prince (Forced proximity)

Forgotten Prince (mariage pact)

Stolen Crown (brother's best friend)

Related short story: Reckless in Ruins

Roadside Attractions series:

Roadside Attraction (insta love)

Claiming Fate (rivals to lovers)

Falling into Fate (long lost friends to lovers)

Fate's Dark Shadows (age gap)

Rode Hard (insta love, dating app)

Crash into Me (grumpy mountain man)

Snowed Under (second chance, later-in-life)

Wish List (holiday, older heroine/younger hero)

Fate's Holi-Date (he falls first, age gap)

Wood Brothers series

(OTT alpha insta-love. Set in same world as Roadside Attractions.)

Nailed

Screwed

Drilled

Love Games series

(OTT insta love, nerdy-but-hot heroes. Set in same world as Roadside Attractions.)

Roll For Initiative

Roll for Damage

Roll for Charisma

Paradise Passions

(vacation romances)

Babymoon

Honeymoon Hideout

Holiday short reads

Elf-napped

Bagged by the Elf

Wish List

Snow-plowed

The Christmas Pickup

The Halloween Bet

The Halloween Flip

Pumpkin King

Snow-plowed

Additional titles are available on iBooks, Barnes & Noble, Everand, Smashwords, Fable, and more.

For signed paperbacks, exclusive downloads, and more, visit Abby's website at authorabbyknox.com

Happy reading!

ABOUT THE AUTHOR

Abby Knox writes feel-good, high-heat romance that readers have described as quirky, sexy, adorable, and hilarious.

Abby's favorite tropes include: Forced proximity, opposites attract, grumpy/sunshine, age gap, boss/employee, fated mates/insta-love, and more. Abby is heavily influenced by Buffy the Vampire Slayer, Gilmore Girls, and LOST. But don't worry, she won't ever make you suffer like Luke & Lorelai.

Say hello at authorabbyknox@gmail.com

And don't forget to visit Abby's website at www.authorabbyknox.com to subscribe to the newsletter to stay on top of all the latest news and get FREE stuff!